The Cool Club

Look for more

titles:

TWO of a kind ™

The Cool Club

adapted by Judy Katschke

from the series created by
Robert Griffard
& Howard Adler

■ HarperEntertainment
An Imprint of HarperCollinsPublishers

A PARACHUTE PRESS BOOK

A PARACHUTE PRESS BOOK

Parachute Publishing, L.L.C.
156 Fifth Avenue
Suite 302
New York, NY 10010

Published by
☰HarperEntertainment

An Imprint of HarperCollins*Publishers*
10 East 53rd Street, New York, NY 10022-5299

TWO OF A KIND books created and produced by
Parachute Press, L.C.C., in cooperation with Dualstar Publications,
a division of Dualstar Entertainment Group, Inc.
published by HarperEntertainment, an imprint of
HarperCollins Publishers
Cover photograph courtesy of Dualstar Entertainment Group, Inc.© 2000

For information address HarperCollins Publishers,
10 East 53rd Street, New York, NY 10022-5299.

ISBN 0-06-106582-X

First printing: August 2000

Printed in the United States of America

Visit HarperEntertainment on the World Wide Web at
www.harpercollins.com

10 9 8 7 6 5 4 3 2 1

CHAPTER ONE

"I don't get it, Ashley," Mary-Kate Burke told her sister. "If we're twins, how come you cook like a pro and all I can make is instant pudding?"

"For the same reason you toss a softball like a pro," Ashley said. "And all I can toss—is a salad!"

"Whatever." Mary-Kate shrugged as she cracked an egg. "I'm just counting on you to get me through this class!"

Ashley blew flour from her strawberry-blond bangs and kneaded her oatmeal cookie dough. It was Monday and the start of the fall semester at the White Oak Academy for Girls. She and Mary-Kate had begun boarding school last winter, while their father was away on a research trip—to study bugs in the Amazon! Kevin Burke was a science professor and had taken care of the girls since their mother died three years ago.

When the girls returned in the fall, they felt right at home. They shared friends and even some classes. One of those classes was cooking.

"It's not *cooking*!" their friend Wendy Linden had told them when they got their schedules. "It's *Culinary Arts*!"

"And it's not in a *kitchen*," Mary-Kate's roommate Campbell Smith had corrected. "It's at the *Food Management Center*."

Okay, okay. So maybe there were a few things they still had to get used to. Like calling the seventh grade the First Form! But as long as Ashley could cook up a storm, she didn't mind what they called it!

Ashley glanced around the shiny classroom with the stainless-steel workstations. Dana Woletsky looked grossed out as she greased her cookie sheet. Campbell was eating more raisins than she put into the mix. Wendy had more flour on her face than on her dough, and Phoebe Cahill was tying a pink-and-orange apron around her waist.

"It's vintage 1971!" Phoebe was telling her cooking buddy. "With an original cheese fondue stain!"

Ashley wasn't surprised. All of her roommate's

clothes were vintage—another word for old!

"You're the one for me, one for me, one for meeee," Mary-Kate began humming under her breath.

Ashley bit her lip. Mary-Kate was at it again— humming the song "In Your Face" by their favorite group, 4-You!

The twins had tried to get tickets to the 4-You Chicago concert over Christmas break. But even though they had practically camped out at the ticket line—the concert was all sold out!

"Quit it, Mary-Kate!" Ashley pleaded.

"But I thought you loved that song!" Mary-Kate said.

"That's the problem!" Ashley said. "You know we can't get tickets for the concert. So quit torturing me!" She reached for the raisins when she heard another sound—a loud, snorting sound.

Whirling around, she saw Arthur and Andrew Nunzio from the Harrington School for Boys. The gross twins were not the boys Ashley was hoping to have in their cooking class!

"Mary-Kate!" Ashley whispered.

"Now what?" Mary-Kate cried, giving her dough a whack.

"The Nunzio twins are shoving cinnamon sticks

up their noses!" Ashley complained. "They give twins a bad name!"

"Ignore them." Mary-Kate sighed. "And stay away from the cinnamon sticks."

Ashley continued to add her cookie ingredients. She wasn't surprised they were baking oatmeal cookies. Oatmeal for breakfast had been a White Oak tradition since 1896!

"Okay, class!" Their cooking teacher, Ms. Nesbitt, clapped her floury hands for attention. "Our ovens are preheating. Which means you should be ready to roll! Now, remember." She grinned as she patted down her crisp white apron. "The best baker in this class will be chosen to make a cake for Mrs. Pritchard's tea on Saturday. And we know how important *that* is!"

Whispers filled the classroom. Mrs. Pritchard was the headmistress—better known as "the Head"—at White Oak.

"I'm putting my money on you, Ashley," Mary-Kate whispered. "You've already aced this class."

"Who . . . me?" Ashley asked modestly. But deep inside she knew that her lemon squares were luscious! Her brownies breathtaking! And her coconut custard tarts—

"Ugh—gross!" Mary-Kate interrupted Ashley's

thoughts. "I just found something skeevy in my dough!"

"A hair?" Ashley gasped. "Please don't tell Ms. Nesbitt—or she'll make us wear *hairnets*!"

"Not a hair," Mary-Kate said, pointing to her slab of dough. "Glitter. Blue glitter, to be exact."

Ashley checked out Mary-Kate's dough. Her sister was right. Her globe of dough sparkled like a disco ball!

"Where did that come from?" Ashley asked.

"Where else?" Mary-Kate asked. "Elise Van Hook is wearing blue glitter on her cheeks. She must be leaking!"

Elise? Ashley glanced back at Elise Van Hook.

Elise was the cool new girl at White Oak. She had a full entertainment center in her room and a serious wardrobe. She also had brown hair and brown eyes—and a passion for glitter!

But it wasn't just Elise's clothes that made her cool. The buzz was that Elise was a blast to be around. She shared yummy snacks from her microwave oven and had parties in her room with crazy themes. She was also great at making everyone laugh. Not bad for a new kid!

"What are you going to do?" Ashley asked as Mary-Kate scooped up Exhibit A in her hands.

"I'm going to tell Miss Pixie Dust to keep her glitter to herself!" Mary-Kate growled.

"No, Mary-Kate!" Ashley protested. "Elise is . . . cool!"

"I don't care how cool she is," Mary-Kate said. "I'm going to give her a piece of my mind."

Ashley ran after her sister, but it was no use. Mary-Kate had already plunked her dough ball in front of Elise.

"Look at that ball of dough!" Mary-Kate said.

Elise tilted her head as she examined the dough. "What's wrong with it?" she asked.

"It's oozing with your glitter, that's what's wrong with it," Mary-Kate repeated. She pointed to her ball of dough. "I want to bake this stuff—not drop it on Times Square!"

Elise blushed a bit. She was also wearing a glitter headband and sparkly crystal earrings. "Sorry." She sighed. "I guess I kind of like to stand out."

"Stand out?" Mary-Kate scoffed. "You practically light up the whole state of New Hampshire!"

"I'm sure she means that as a compliment," Ashley said to Elise. She tugged at Mary-Kate's elbow. "Come on, Mary-Kate. Time to grease our cookie sheets—"

"Wait!" Elise interrupted. She gave the twins a

warm smile. "Would you guys like to eat lunch at my table today? We can get to know each other better—and you can meet some of my other new friends."

Ashley dropped Mary-Kate's elbow. They were just invited to sit with the newest most popular girl at White Oak. How could they say no?

"We'd love to!" Ashley blurted.

She felt Mary-Kate tug her aside. "Ashley," she muttered. "We always eat lunch with Campbell, Phoebe, and Wendy. Remember?"

"So they can join us," Ashley whispered back. She gave Elise a thumbs-up sign. "Thanks, we'll be there!"

"Cool!" Elise said. She picked up Mary-Kate's dough ball and tossed it. "Here—catch!"

Mary-Kate made a perfect catch. Ashley was about to turn away when she noticed Dana Woletsky glaring at Elise with fire in her eyes. What was *her* problem?

"Come on," Mary-Kate told Ashley. "Let's get back to work. Before we flunk Oatmeal Cookies 101!"

"Do you believe it?" Ashley squealed as they hurried back to their workstations. "We just made friends with the newest cool girl at White Oak!"

"Sounds familiar." Mary-Kate pressed her palm

into her ball of dough. "You said the same thing when you cozied up to Dana Woletsky."

Ashley rolled her eyes. "Do you have to remind me?" She groaned.

She used to think Dana was the coolest girl in the First Form. Dana had long, shiny brown hair and clothes to die for. But then the twins found out she could make their lives miserable. Like the time Dana pushed Ashley to write a gossipy article about Mary-Kate for the school newspaper. When Ashley tried to take it back, Dana went ahead and printed it!

"Dana is yesterday's news." Ashley sighed as she turned back to her cookies. "*Bad* news!"

"Don't let her hear you say that," Mary-Kate warned, looking over her shoulder. "She might . . . she might . . ."

"She might what, Mary-Kate?" Ashley asked.

Mary-Kate turned to Ashley with wide eyes. "Ashley, you're not going to believe what I just saw!" she whispered.

"What?" Ashley whispered back.

"Dana Woletsky just dumped something into Elise's cookie dough!"

CHAPTER TWO

"No way!" Ashley cried. "It could have been poison! Or something yucky from the biology lab!"

"Nah," Mary-Kate said. "The bottle was from the spice rack. I doubt Ms. Nesbitt keeps poison next to the nutmeg and cinnamon."

Ashley breathed a sigh of relief.

"Whatever it was, Dana probably ruined Elise's cookies," Mary-Kate said. "Why would she do that?"

"Who knows," Ashley said. "But we have to warn Elise. Before Ms. Nesbitt tastes her cookies—and gags!"

But it was too late. Elise was already sliding her tainted cookies into the big industrial oven.

When all of the cookies were baking, Mary-Kate and Ashley pulled Elise aside. "Dana Woletsky sabotaged your cookie dough," Mary-Kate whispered. "She dumped something in it when you weren't looking."

Mary-Kate expected Elise to flip—but instead she acted cool. "I'm not surprised," she said. "It's probably because of Summer Sorenson."

"Summer?" the twins repeated at the same time. Summer was a First Form girl from Malibu Beach, California. She was friendly, blond, and had a tan that never seemed to fade. She was also a bit spacy. Ashley thought it must be from spending so much time in the sun without a hat!

"Summer used to be one of Dana's best friends," Elise said. "Until she started hanging out with me."

"Bummer," Mary-Kate told Elise.

They all looked back at Dana. She was busy talking to some Harrington boys—and acting like nothing had happened!

"Sorry we couldn't stop her, Elise," Ashley said.

"That's okay," Elise said. She narrowed her eyes at Dana. "I may be new at White Oak, but I know how to handle Dana Woletsky!"

Ping!

The girls jumped when Ms. Nesbitt's timer went off.

10

"Time to take our cookies out of the oven!" Ms. Nesbitt announced. "And time for the big taste test!"

Mary-Kate and Ashley joined the others as they carried their cookie trays from the ovens to their workstations.

"I hope Ms. Nesbitt likes glitter as much as she likes anchovies!" Mary-Kate whispered to Ashley.

Ms. Nesbitt approached Ashley's tray first and reached for a cookie. "Mmm-mmm!" she said as she chewed. "This is an ambitious oatmeal cookie, Ashley. Can you tell us what secret ingredient you used?"

Mary-Kate shot Ashley a glance. No way would she reveal her secret recipe to anyone.

"Secret ingredient?" Ashley gulped. "Um . . . I doubled up on . . . lemon zest."

"Lemon zest? In oatmeal cookies?" Ms. Nesbitt asked. "Oh, well. You must be doing something right, Ashley."

Mary-Kate expected Mrs. Nesbitt to taste her cookies next, but instead she walked over to Elise.

"Uh-oh," Mary-Kate whispered. "Gag alert!"

Mrs. Nesbitt took a bite out of Elise's cookie. But even before she started to chew—she sputtered!

"Since when do we bake oatmeal cookies with pepper, Elise?" she demanded. "I'm afraid this is a definite NH."

Mary-Kate gulped. They didn't get regular grades at White Oak. But an NH for "Needs Help" might as well be an F.

Mary-Kate was sure Elise would tell Mrs. Nesbitt all about Dana. But while Ms. Nesbitt was busy with another student, Elise sealed one cookie into a plastic bag. Then she stormed over to Dana and waved the bag in her face.

"I know *you* dumped pepper in my cookies, Dana!" Mary-Kate heard Elise say. "And I can bust you anytime—just remember that!"

"Give me a break," Dana groaned. "That cookie is no proof that I did it."

"Who needs proof?" Elise nodded over at Mary-Kate. "I have something better. A *witness*!"

Dana spun around and glared at Mary-Kate. Then she flipped her hair over her shoulders and huffed away.

"Let's see her try *that* again," Elise said, swinging the plastic bag. "Thanks, guys."

Mary-Kate stared at Elise as she returned to her workstation. "Boy, was I wrong about Elise!" she said. "She is one tough cookie!"

Ashley took a nibble of Mary-Kate's oatmeal cookie. Her eyes practically crossed as she gulped it down. "So is *this*, Mary-Kate," she cried. "I think you'd better stick to instant pudding!"

Mary-Kate tasted her own cookie and frowned. "I think you're right!" She sighed.

"Why can't we just eat at our regular lunch table?" Wendy asked the twins later in the dining hall. The girls were carrying trays filled with grilled cheese sandwiches and hot tuna casseroles.

"Because change is good," Ashley said. "And we happen to have a special invitation to eat with Elise Van Hook!"

"Uh-oh," Campbell joked. "I hope you like your grilled cheese with glitter!"

"Oh, come on, you guys," Ashley said. "You'll like Elise—she's really nice!"

Elise waved from the back of the dining room. She was sitting at a round table under the portraits of the White Oak headmistresses. "Yoo-hoo!" she called. "Over heeeeere!"

As they walked closer, Mary-Kate saw three other First Form girls at Elise's table. They were Summer Sorenson, Cheryl Miller, and Elise's roommate, Samantha Kramer.

Mary-Kate was happy to see Cheryl. Cheryl was always fun to be around. But then Mary-Kate

13

noticed something else . . .

"Check it out," Mary-Kate said. "They're all wearing blue glitter. On their hair, their cheeks—"

"I know!" Ashley said excitedly. "It must be the latest fashion trend."

"Hi, Elise," Ashley said. "Meet Wendy Linden, Phoebe Cahill, and Campbell Smith."

Elise looked surprised. "Oh, wow!" she said. "If I had known you were all coming I would have saved more seats. There's only two—for Mary-Kate and Ashley!"

"Can we move to a bigger table?" Ashley asked.

Elise looked at her friends and giggled. "And leave Harvey?" she asked.

"Harvey?" Mary-Kate asked. "Who's Harvey?"

Elise pointed to the ceiling. Mary-Kate glanced up at one of the stone gargoyles. "Harvey" had wings and was grinning down at them with sharp fangs!

Elise's friends broke out into fits of giggles. Mary-Kate wanted to laugh, too. Elise was definitely a character.

"I have an idea," Ashley said. "Let's pull up some more chairs."

Campbell shook her head. "It's cool, Ashley," she said. "You and Mary-Kate stay here. We'll go to our regular table."

"Yeah." Wendy smiled at Elise. "The one under the gargoyle we call Clarence!"

Mary-Kate watched Phoebe, Wendy, and Campbell walk away. *Oh, well*, she thought. *It's just for one day. And they don't seem to mind.*

After dusting glitter off of their chairs, Mary-Kate and Ashley sat down with their trays.

"We were just talking about Elise's new DVD player!" Cheryl said. "We're going to her room tonight to watch a movie on it!"

"*Our* room," Samantha said. She put her arm around Elise's shoulders. "I'm Elise's roommate, you know."

"A DVD player—cool!" Mary-Kate said. She was about to take a bite of her sandwich when Elise grabbed her hand.

"Save that for a midnight snack," Elise said. She pointed to a big plastic container on the table. "I made some burritos in my microwave—for all of us!"

"Did you say . . . burritos?" Mary-Kate asked. She would walk a mile on her hands for a good burrito!

"Guacamole and chicken," Elise said, handing them out. "Mealtime should be fun-time, don't you think?"

Mary-Kate smiled as she took a chicken burrito.

"Last week Elise made us some chili," Cheryl

15

volunteered. "We had a contest to see who could eat the most with a pair of chopsticks."

"I'll bet my parents are experts at eating with chopsticks," Elise said. "They've been in Japan for over a month now."

"Japan?" Ashley asked. "What are they doing there?"

Elise shrugged. "They're rock concert promoters. Right now they're in Tokyo with 4-You."

Clunk! Ashley dropped her burrito on her plate. "4-You?" she squealed. "They're our favorite group!"

"We tried to get tickets for their Chicago concert," Mary-Kate said. "But they were sold out!"

"Bummer," Elise said. "It helps if you know someone in the biz. Like my parents."

Mary-Kate felt Ashley squeeze her arm under the table. She knew Ashley wanted to ask Elise for tickets, but Mary-Kate shook her head. They hardly knew Elise!

Ashley chewed on her burrito. Then her eyes lit up. "You know, Elise, your parents would make a great story! I'm a reporter for the school paper, the *Acorn*. Maybe I can write an article all about you and your supercool mom and dad!"

Elise shook Ashley's arm. "Front page?"

"Don't know yet," Ashley admitted. "I have to run the idea by Phoebe. She was just promoted to

First Form editor. But she always likes my ideas!"

Elise pumped her fist in the air. "That would be great!" she cheered.

But Mary-Kate wasn't so sure. "You'd better rethink this, Elise," she said. "Once that story comes out, *everyone* will want tickets!"

Elise shook her head. She leaned over and began to whisper. "I only get tickets for members of"—she looked around—"my club."

"Club?" Ashley asked. "What . . . club?"

"The Glitter Girls!" Elise said excitedly.

Mary-Kate raised an eyebrow as she drank her cranberry juice. So *that* explained all that glitter!

"We're all members!" Samantha said. "Elise promised to get the Backstreet Boys to sing at my bat mitzvah. But then again, I *am* her roommate!"

"And Elise lets us borrow anything from her closet," Summer said. "Except underwear, of course."

"And every week we meet in her room to watch her big-screen TV!" Cheryl said.

"What a totally awesome club!" Ashley cried.

"It *is* awesome," Elise agreed. She tilted her head and grinned. "Now . . . how would you two like to join?"

CHAPTER THREE

"You mean become Glitter Girls?" Ashley cried.

"Shh," Elise said, putting her finger to her lips. "I have just given you top-secret information!"

"Okay, okay," Mary-Kate whispered. "But what makes a Glitter Girl . . . a Glitter Girl?"

Elise counted on her glitter-nail-polished fingers.

"For one, they eat all their meals together, at least for the first week," she explained. "And of course they wear glitter!"

"That means a different color every day," Summer said. She took out a small vial of blue glitter. "Today is Monday, so the color is Bodacious Blue!"

But Ashley wasn't thinking of glitter. She was

thinking of the 4-You concert over Christmas break!

"Elise?" Ashley asked slowly. "Not that this will determine whether I join the Glitter Girls or not, but will members be getting tickets to . . . 4-You?"

"Why not?" Elise giggled as she pointed to each girl. "I'll get tickets 4-you, and 4-you, and 4-*you*!"

"Where do we sign up?" Ashley blurted.

"Wait, Ashley." Mary-Kate turned to the other girls. "Are secret clubs even allowed here at White Oak?"

"Clubs are," Cheryl said. "Initiations aren't."

"Yes they are," Summer said sweetly. "My initiations are on my towels. They're S.V.S. Summer Victoria—"

"Those are *initials*, Summer," Cheryl groaned.

"Oh," Summer said, wrinkling her nose.

"Initiations are when you have to do silly or dangerous things to join a club," Mary-Kate explained. "Campbell told me that years ago a bunch of Second Formers started a club here with initiations. When the Head found out, they were grounded from activities for a whole month!"

"A whole month?" Cheryl shuddered. "We don't *want* to have to worry about initiations."

"Yeah." Elise shook her head. "We don't go there."

"Then everything's cool," Ashley said. She gave

Mary-Kate a grin. "What do you say, Mary-Kate? Are you in?"

"It all depends." Mary-Kate turned to Elise. "Can Campbell, Wendy, and Phoebe join the club, too?"

Silence.

Elise finally laughed. "Whoa! One pledge at a time. Or in your case . . . two!"

Ashley wasn't worried. She was sure Elise would ask their friends to join, too. Eventually.

"In the meantime," Elise warned, "you have to promise not to tell anyone about this club." She gave an excited wiggle. "Now for the fun part. You both have to meet us in back of the Computer Center!"

"What for?" Ashley asked.

"To learn the club rules!" Elise replied.

"Okay," Mary-Kate said. "When should we be there? During midday break? Before dinner?"

The Glitter Girls giggled.

"After *lights out!*" Elise declared.

"No way!" Ashley cried. "Mr. Cameron, the night guard, watches Porter House like a pit bull!"

"I'll think of something, Ashley," Mary-Kate said. "Just meet me outside your door at ten o'clock tonight."

"And wear glitter!" Samantha added.

Mary-Kate dusted a clump of Bodacious Blue glitter from her sleeve. "I already am!" she joked.

"Phoebe?" Ashley asked that evening in her room. "I just had an awesome idea for the next edition!"

Phoebe was sitting on her bed and checking proofs for an article she was writing. "Really?" She peeked over her glasses. "What?"

Ashley hopped on her own bed and stared at Phoebe. "I want to write an article about Elise Van Hook," she said. "Her mom and dad are concert promoters. They travel all over the world with the hottest rock groups!"

Phoebe kicked off her seventies platform shoes. "We already did a story like that the semester before you came," she said. "Felicia O'Donnell's parents promote concerts, too."

"Oh," Ashley said, disappointed.

"Sorry, Ashley," Phoebe said, going back to her proofs. "But your story just isn't special enough."

Not special enough?

Ashley didn't get it. Phoebe always loved her ideas—even if they couldn't use them.

So why was she acting so weird?

CHAPTER FOUR

"Did you bring a flashlight?" Ashley whispered in the hallway that night.

"Nope," Mary-Kate whispered back. "Why?"

"It's dark outside," Ashley replied. "We need it to find Elise and her friends behind the Computer Center."

"Ashley, get real," Mary-Kate joked. "They're the Glitter Girls! How can we miss them?"

Mary-Kate looked up and down the hall to see if the coast was clear. Then, very quietly, the twins made their way down the staircase.

Luckily the stairwell door didn't creak as Mary-Kate opened it. Peeking out, she could see Mr. Cameron sitting in the lobby. He was busy watching a game show on a tiny TV set on his desk.

"Don't be a wimp!" Mr. Cameron shouted at the TV set. "Go for the million bucks! Go for the million bucks!"

"Mary-Kate, there is no way we are going to sneak out of the dorm," Ashley whispered. "Mr. Cameron guards the main door *and* the side door!"

Mary-Kate smiled as she glanced at her watch. If her plan worked, the doorbell would be ringing just about now.

"Five, four, three," Mary-Kate began to count down.

"What are you doing?" Ashley hissed.

Ring! The main doorbell rang. Mr. Cameron looked puzzled as he stood up and opened the door.

"Pizza delivery for Ralph Cameron," a boy with a blue jacket and hat said. He held out a big flat box.

"Pizza?" Mr. Cameron shook his head. "Why, I didn't order a pizza!"

Mary-Kate grinned at Ashley. "How do you like that?" she asked. "Pizza Palace *does* deliver exactly on time!"

"Good thinking, Mary-Kate!" Ashley grinned.

Mr. Cameron was still arguing with the pizza boy as the twins slipped out the side door. Once outside, Mary-Kate yanked the hood of her sweatshirt over her head. It was late September, and the nights were getting cool.

"All systems go!" she told Ashley.

They scurried away from Porter House toward the Computer Center. The stars were bright enough to light the way.

"Where are they?" Mary-Kate asked Ashley when they reached the big glass and brick building. "They said—"

"Greetings, pledges!" Elise's voice interrupted.

Mary-Kate whirled around. The Glitter Girls were stepping out from behind the building and the shadows.

Elise's brown hair was pulled back into two braids. Her eyelids were coated with purple-glitter eye shadow, and her lips sparkled with a glittery pink gloss. Summer, Cheryl, and Samantha wore glitter headbands and glitter makeup, too.

Forget the flashlights, Mary-Kate thought with a smile. *I should have worn shades!*

"Hey, guys!" Ashley said.

"Hi," Elise said quickly. "Ashley, what did Phoebe say about the article about me and my parents?"

Ashley sighed. "I don't know how to tell you this, Elise, but Phoebe nixed the idea."

Mary-Kate expected Elise to be angry about the article, but instead she smiled and gave a little shrug.

"Oh, well," Elise said. "It's Phoebe's loss."

Mary-Kate shivered. The breeze was getting brisk. "Can we cut to the chase here?" she asked Elise. "Before my knees turn into snow globes?"

"Okay, okay," Elise said. "Let's all join hands and recite the Glitter Girls oath!"

Mary-Kate felt like giggling as they joined hands. She hadn't taken an oath since she joined the Girl Scouts!

"We have gathered tonight as the secret society of Glitter Girls!" Elise announced. "Shine, shine, glimmer, glimmer! Power glows where we shimmer!"

This is wild! Mary-Kate thought. *Wait until Campbell, Wendy, and Phoebe join up—they'll dig it!*

After the oath, Elise explained the rules: "Rule number one: Never, ever talk about Glitter Girls! Rule number two: Always wear glitter every day!"

Ashley held up her hands. She was wearing pink-glitter nail polish. "Ta-daaa!" she said. "I'm way ahead of you!"

"Nice start, Ashley," Elise said. She reached into her pocket and pulled out a small clear plastic bag filled with Bodacious Blue glitter. "But that's just the beginning!"

Mary-Kate watched as Elise reached into the bag and pinched a clump of glitter between her fingers.

"Prepare to be anointed!" Elise declared. She reached out and sprinkled the blue glitter over Mary-Kate's and Ashley's heads. "Arise, Glitter Girls, arise!"

"Easy with that stuff!" Mary-Kate coughed as some glitter flew up her nostrils. She liked Elise and she liked the club—but the glitter she could do without!

As for Ashley, she seemed to love it. "Look at me! I'm a Glitter Girl!" she squealed. "I'm a Glitter Girl!"

"Not so fast!" Elise laughed. "You're not a full-fledged member until you go through a week of special challenges."

Mary-Kate and Ashley looked at each other.

"Challenges?" Mary-Kate said. "But you said you guys don't do initiations."

"And we don't!" Cheryl insisted.

"Here's how it works," Elise explained. "You'll receive your daily challenge every morning during breakfast. But since this is a special night, I'll give you your challenge right now!"

Elise nodded at Summer and Samantha. The two girls held up two jars—one with peanut butter, one with dill pickles.

"Come to breakfast tomorrow with peanut butter face-masks," Elise said. "And roll your hair with pickles!"

"Are you serious?" Mary-Kate laughed. Where did Elise come up with these crazy ideas? But Ashley wasn't laughing.

"No way will I do that!" Ashley declared. "No way will I put peanut butter on my face!"

Mary-Kate grabbed the peanut butter. "Oh, lighten up, Ashley!" she said. "All this stuff is just goofy fun."

"Peanut butter is for crackers, Mary-Kate," Ashley said. "Not my face."

Cheryl began to sing softly: "Every party has a pooper that's why we invited you. Party pooper . . ."

Mary-Kate began to panic. There had to be a way to make Ashley change her mind. Maybe there was.

"You know," Mary-Kate said slowly. "I'm sure all that peanut butter will wash off in time for the 4-You concert."

"The 4-You concert?" Ashley gasped.

"Chicago," Mary-Kate went on. "Christmas break . . ."

"Give me that pickle jar!" Ashley told Samantha.

It worked! Mary-Kate thought.

"Okay, Glitter Girls!" Elise said: "Let's split up and

walk back to our houses. And remember our motto . . ."

The Glitter Girls gave each other thumbs-up signs. "You glow, girl!" they chanted.

"You glow, girl!" Mary-Kate said. "Cute!"

The twins said good night to the Glitter Girls and headed back to Porter House.

"Elise Van Hook is such a blast!" Mary-Kate said as they hurried along the path. "Do you believe I'm actually *glad* she leaked glitter into my cookie dough?"

"And I can't believe we sneaked out in the middle of the night!" Ashley squealed.

"Yeah," Mary-Kate said. "Now if I can just figure out how to sneak back *in*!"

As they walked a few more feet, Mary-Kate glanced up at Phipps House, another First Form dorm. A girl was standing at one of the lighted windows and watching them.

Mary-Kate stopped walking and looked closer.

The girl was Dana Woletsky!

Oh, great, Mary-Kate thought. *All Dana has to do is tell Mrs. Pritchard that we were sneaking outside after lights out.*

We'll be toast!

CHAPTER FIVE

"I wish I could disappear," Ashley groaned to Mary-Kate the next morning in the dining hall. She could feel her peanut butter mask hardening on her face.

"Don't think about the peanut butter," Mary-Kate whispered as they pushed their trays along the serving line. "Just keep thinking about those 4-You tickets!"

Ashley nodded. When she said she'd do anything for 4-You tickets, she wasn't kidding!

"Keep the line moving!" Mrs. Bromsky, the dining hall lady, shouted. When she saw the twins, her mouth dropped open like a trapdoor. "What happened to you two?"

Ashley gulped. They couldn't tell anyone about their special challenge. So she thought of something—fast!

"It's the latest beauty treatment from Hollywood, Mrs. Bromsky!" Ashley said. "The peanut butter is supposed to make your skin smooth and supple."

"What about the pickles on your heads?" Mrs. Bromsky asked. "What's that supposed to do?"

"Um," Ashley said. She forced herself to smile. "It keeps you cool as a cucumber!"

Mrs. Bromsky raised an eyebrow as she slid two bowls of oatmeal toward the twins. "Kids," she muttered.

Ashley picked up her tray.

The twins carried their trays a few feet when Ashley heard a familiar voice. . . .

"You two have got to be kidding!"

Spinning around, Ashley saw Wendy standing with Phoebe and Campbell. They were all holding trays and staring at the twins with wide eyes.

"You look totally gross!" Wendy gasped.

Ashley tried to smile. She could feel the peanut butter crack around her mouth. "We may look gross now, but after we wash our faces we'll look totally glam!" she said.

"That is *outrageous*!" Phoebe said, shaking her head.

"No it's not," Mary-Kate joked. "It's extra-chunky!"

Ashley wished she could tell her friends about the Glitter Girls, but she knew she couldn't. Not yet!

"Why don't you wash that goop off and come to our table?" Wendy said. "I just got my summer vacation pictures, and I'm dying to show you the boy I liked."

Ashley was about to say yes when she remembered something—she and Mary-Kate had to eat breakfast with the Glitter Girls.

"Um," Ashley said, "we can't eat with you today."

"Why not?" Phoebe asked.

"Mary-Kate! Ashley!" Elise gave a friendly wave from her table. "I've saved two seats."

"*Two* seats?" Wendy cried. "Again?"

"So that's it," Campbell said. "You'd rather sit with Elise and her friends than with us."

Mary-Kate's pickle rollers wiggled as she shook her head. "No!" she said. "It's just—"

"It's just that Elise is helping us with a particular subject!" Ashley broke in.

"What?" Campbell asked angrily. "*Ditching?*"

The word hit Ashley like a ton of bricks. The last

thing she wanted to do was ditch her friends.

"Let's go, Wendy," Phoebe said. "*I* want to see your summer vacation pictures."

"And that cute guy, too," Campbell said.

A clump of peanut butter dripped off of Ashley's nose as she watched her friends walk away.

"Maybe we *should* eat with them," Mary-Kate said. "Elise is cool—she'd understand."

But Ashley didn't want anything to spoil their chances of becoming Glitter Girls. And of getting 4-You tickets.

"They'll get over it," Ashley assured her. "Especially when Elise asks them to join."

More girls whispered and giggled as the twins carried their trays to the Glitter Girls table. Ashley was sure that Harvey the gargoyle was having a good laugh, too!

"Congratulations!" Elise said as Mary-Kate and Ashley sat down. "You passed your very first challenge!"

Summer picked up a phial of green glitter and handed it to Ashley. "So you get a touch of Tuesday's color. Groovy Green!" she said.

Ashley opened the vial and dotted some glitter on her hands. "Want some, Mary-Kate?" she asked.

Mary-Kate shook her head. "I just want to know

one thing: When can Campbell, Wendy, and Phoebe join?"

"Here we go again," Cheryl said, rolling her dark brown eyes.

"You'd like Campbell—she's a great athlete," Mary-Kate said. "In fact, we have softball practice right after classes today."

"Today?" Elise shook her head. "Oh, but you can't practice today. You and Ashley have too much work to do!"

"Work?" Ashley asked. "What kind of work?"

The Glitter Girls exchanged looks and giggled. Elise took a sip of milk and wiggled closer to the twins.

"Some boys from Harrington are coming to White Oak after classes," she said. "For glee club!"

Boys! Ashley immediately thought of Ross Lambert. Ross was the boy at Harrington she had a serious crush on.

"Two of those boys are Arthur and Andrew Nunzio!" Elise went on.

Ashley gasped. "You mean the gross Nunzio twins?"

"What do they have to do with us?" Mary-Kate asked.

"That's your next challenge!" Elise exclaimed. "You and Ashley have to slip the twins a love note signed with your names. Is that a major hoot or what?"

"But we don't even like those boys!" Mary-Kate said.

"And I already have a boyfriend," Ashley said, thinking of Ross. "Well . . . I think I do."

"You *hope* you do!" Mary-Kate murmured.

"It's up to you." Elise shrugged. She turned to Summer, Samantha, and Cheryl. "Check it out. They're having a 4-You video marathon on TV tonight. I thought we could watch it on my big-screen TV."

"Can we sit in your beanbag chairs?" Summer asked.

"And make popcorn in your microwave?" Cheryl asked.

"Sure," Elise said. She rubbed her hands together.

Beanbag chairs! A 4-You marathon on a big-screen TV! Ashley thought. *Elise's room is the ultimate clubhouse. And the Glitter Girls is the ultimate club. Mary-Kate and I have to join!*

"Okay, we'll do it!" Ashley cried. "We'll wow those Nunzio twins!"

"You can wash that stuff off now," Elise told Mary-Kate and Ashley. "You already passed your challenge."

The girls stood up and marched past the pointing, whispering students. But just as they were about to leave the dining hall, Dana moved in front of the door. Her best friend, Kristin Lindquist, was standing at her side.

"Hi, Dana," Mary-Kate said. "What's up?"

Dana folded her arms across her chest. "I don't know what the peanut butter is all about," she said. "But I saw you sneaking around last night after lights out!"

Ashley felt her blood freeze. She saw Mary-Kate taking a few steps forward.

"And I saw you dump pepper into Elise's cookie dough," Mary-Kate shot back. She gave Dana a small smile. "So if you're thinking of telling Mrs. Pritchard about last night . . . think again."

Dana narrowed her eyes at Mary-Kate. Then she turned to Kristin. "Come on, Kristin," she said. "This place reeks of peanut butter and pickles!"

"Did you really do it, Dana?" Kristin asked as she followed Dana out of the dining hall. "Did you really trash Elise's cookies?"

The twins waited until Dana was gone.

"That takes care of her," Mary-Kate said.

But Ashley wasn't so sure.

Dana has caused plenty of trouble for us before, she thought. *Will she do it again?*

CHAPTER SIX

"Ashley?" Mary-Kate called as she knocked on her sister's door. "Are you in? Open up!"

"It's open," Ashley called back from inside.

Mary-Kate opened the door to peek in, then stepped back with a gasp. The room was totally clouded with a sparkly mist!

"It's called Blue Moon Dust!" Ashley said as she patted her arms with a sparkly blue powder puff. "I only use it when Phoebe's not around. She doesn't really like glitter."

Mary-Kate gave a little cough. "I wonder why!"

Ashley placed the puff back in the round cardboard box. "Now I feel like a true Glitter Girl," she said, her arms sparkling. "Let's get to work!"

"Ashley, I think Elise is cool, and I want to join the Glitter Girls," Mary-Kate groaned. "But I do *not* want to write a love note to the Nunzio twins!"

"Don't think of it as a love note!" Ashley said. "Think of it—as a ticket to the 4-You concert!"

Mary-Kate smiled. "Well, if you put it that way . . . "

Ashley sat down on her bed and began to bounce. "I thought a love *poem* would be a good idea," she said.

"A poem, huh?" Mary-Kate snapped her fingers. "How's this? Roses are red, violets are blue. We are twins . . . and so are you!"

Ashley rolled her eyes. "That's not a love poem!"

"And I'm not a poet!" Mary-Kate complained. "Look, can't we just copy a poem out of a book?"

"A book?" Ashley repeated. Her eyes suddenly lit up. "How about—a poetry book!"

Mary-Kate watched as Ashley ran over to Phoebe's desk. She gently touched a big cloth-bound book with a lace heart pasted on the cover.

"What's that?" Mary-Kate asked.

"Phoebe's favorite book of poetry," Ashley said. "Half of the poems are about love!" She frowned. "But Phoebe won't let anyone open it. It's an antique!"

Mary-Kate groaned. "Ashley, *everything* Phoebe

owns is an antique. Her toothbrush is probably from 1965!"

"You're right." Ashley sighed, picking up the book. "I'll just be very, very careful."

Mary-Kate peered over Ashley's shoulder as she flipped through the pages. She spotted one designed with red hearts and pink flowers.

"Stop!" Mary-Kate pointed to the page. "That poem looks sappy—I mean—romantic!"

"It's by Elizabeth Barrett Browning." Ashley began to read the poem out loud: "'How do I love thee? Let me count the ways. I love thee to the depth and breadth and height my soul can reach—'"

"I've heard enough," Mary-Kate snapped. "Let's just copy it."

The twins booted up Ashley's computer. After typing the poem and printing it out on flowery stationery, they signed their names.

"Should I spray it with perfume?" Ashley asked.

"How about pest spray?" Mary-Kate joked. She folded the poem into a little square. "Let's get this over with."

The twins ran out of Porter House and across the campus to the Performing Arts Center. Quietly they slipped into the theater. It was filled with students singing the song "Oklahoma" at the top of their lungs.

Mary-Kate spotted Arthur and Andrew sitting in the middle of row J. She and Ashley crouched down low as they inched their way over. Then Mary-Kate tapped the shoulder of a girl sitting in the aisle seat.

"*What?*" the girl whispered.

Mary-Kate shoved the note into her hand. "Pass this note to Arthur and Andrew Nunzio," she whispered back.

The girl shrugged. She passed the note down the row of students until it reached Arthur and Andrew.

"Mission accomplished!" Mary-Kate declared. "Now let's get out of here."

Mary-Kate and Ashley rushed back to Porter House. But as they stepped into Ashley's room, they froze. Phoebe was standing in the middle of the floor with her big book of poetry under her arm. And she looked mad!

"You were going through my antique book of poems, weren't you?" Phoebe demanded.

"H-h-how did you know?" Ashley stammered. Phoebe tipped the book upside down. A flutter of Blue Moon Dust sprinkled down from the pages and onto the floor.

"W-whoops!" Ashley mumbled.

Busted!

CHAPTER SEVEN

"How could you do this, Ashley?" Phoebe asked. "You know how valuable my book is—you could have ruined it!"

"It was an accident, Phoebe," Ashley said. She raised her glittery arms in the air. "I needed a special poem and I must have . . . leaked!"

Phoebe shook her head. "Ever since Elise invited you to her table, you've been acting so weird!"

Ashley sighed. She wished she could explain about the Glitter Girls. All she could do was hope that Phoebe would become a member—soon!

"I'm sorry, Phoebe," Ashley said. "From now on I'll keep my glitter on my side of the room. I promise."

"I didn't know the 4-You drummer had hair up his nose," Mary-Kate said in Elise's room that evening. She turned the brim of her Cubs cap to the front so she could lean against the wall.

The Glitter Girls sat on the floor of Elise's high-tech, state-of-the-art room, munching on chips and staring at her new television set.

"That's the problem with big-screen TVs," Elise said. "You see everything—warts and all."

Ashley smiled as she looked around the room. Elise did have the neatest room. And she was already beginning to feel like a full-fledged Glitter Girl!

"By the way." Elise reached under her bed and pulled out a small vial. It was filled with pink glitter. "The color for tomorrow will be Freaky Fuchsia!"

"Cool!" Mary-Kate said. "I like hot pink."

"Then you'll *love* your next challenge!" Elise laughed.

Mary-Kate raised an eyebrow. "Which is . . . ?"

Elise reached under her bed. She pulled up a small rectangular box of hair dye. *Pink* hair dye!

"I don't like pink *that* much!" Mary-Kate exclaimed.

"Relax!" Elise said. "You only have to wear it for one day. The stuff is temporary. It washes out."

Ashley stared at the model on the hair dye box. She did look kind of funky.

Ashley shrugged. "Pink hair is kind of sweet."

"So is cotton candy!" Mary-Kate said. "Which is what our heads are going to look like after we use this stuff. Sorry, guys. But I'm going to have to pass."

Ashley gasped. Had Mary-Kate forgotten about the 4-You tickets? "It's only for a day," she argued. "Then out it comes!"

Ashley held her breath as Mary-Kate thought it over.

"Okay," Mary-Kate finally said. "I'll do it. But just for twenty-four hours."

"Go for it!" Elise squealed, clapping her hands.

The twins ran to get fresh towels. Then they hurried to the shower room. After shampooing the pink goop into their hair, they stared into the mirrors.

"Didn't we have a My Little Pony this color?" Mary-Kate asked slowly.

Ashley stared at the mirror as she dragged a brush through her hot pink hair. Of all the fashion statements that she ever made—this one screamed the loudest!

"You know, Mary-Kate," Ashley said. "For once I'm glad Dad is all the way in Chicago. The farther away the better."

The door flew open and the twins whirled around. Ashley saw Dana walking into the shower room. She was wearing a flannel robe and carrying a bottle of shampoo.

"Oh my gosh!" Dana said. "Your hair! It's—pink!"

"It's not just pink!" Mary-Kate said cheerfully. She patted her hair. "It's Flaming Flamingo! Do you like it?"

"It's not important what I think," Dana said. "What matters is what Mrs. Pritchard thinks! In case you've forgotten, according to page twelve in the White Oak Academy Student Rules book, all hair color must be a color that grows on the head."

Ashley gulped. She had only gotten to page seven! "You're not going to tell her, are you, Dana?" she asked.

"I don't have to," Dana declared. "Mrs. Pritchard will see for herself. Unless she's color-blind!"

Ashley and Mary-Kate stared at each other.

"I guess I'll come back later." Dana laughed as she turned to leave. "That pink stuff might be contagious!"

The door slammed and Mary-Kate turned to Ashley. "We have to wash this stuff out!" she cried.

"But what about the challenge?" Ashley asked.

"Right now our challenge is Mrs. Pritchard!" Mary-Kate said. She flipped Ashley the bottle of shampoo. "Start lathering!"

The twins jumped back into the showers. But after a brisk shampoo, they noticed that their hair was still pink!

"Elise said it would wash out!" Ashley cried.

"Well, Elise *lied*!" Mary-Kate said.

Ashley stared at Mary-Kate. It was the first bad thing her sister had said about Elise since the blue glitter in the oatmeal cookie batter!

After pulling on their clothes, the twins wrapped towels around their heads and ran back to Elise's room.

"But it *does* wash out," Elise said after the twins showed them their hair. She took the box and read the back. "After about . . . eight shampoos!"

"Eight?" the twins cried.

Summer looked over Elise's shoulder at the box. "It says so in teeny-weeny little letters—"

"Arrrgh!" Mary-Kate groaned, covering her head.

"Oh, noooo!" Ashley cried.

"Okay, okay, okay," Elise said, waving her hands. "I goofed, and I'm sorry. But wait until you see how I'm going to make it up to you!"

"How?" Mary-Kate demanded.

"First of all, starting tomorrow, your challenges will be way different," Elise said. "No more peanut butter, bogus love notes, or pink hair."

"That's good to know." Ashley sighed.

"Second," Elise said. "I'm going to call my parents in Japan tonight. And ask them about tickets to 4-You!"

A shiver of excitement ran down Ashley's back. The tickets were practically in their hands!

"Now, borrow my shampoo and start washing out that Flaming Flamingo," Elise said. "You already washed once, so you only have seven shampoos to go. That's not so bad!"

The twins hurried back to the shower room.

"Mary-Kate, did you hear what she said?" Ashley asked as they ran down the hall. "She's going to ask her mom and dad about tickets! 4-You, here we come!"

"Yeah." Mary-Kate tugged at a strand of hot pink hair. "But I'm beginning to wonder—is it worth it?"

Oh, great, Ashley thought. *The 4-You tickets are practically in our hands. Mary-Kate better not wimp out now!*

CHAPTER
EIGHT

"Pass the sugar, please," Mary-Kate told Ashley the next morning at breakfast.

"What?" Ashley shouted.

"I said, pass the sugar," Mary-Kate repeated.

"*What?*" Ashley shouted again.

"What's wrong with her?" Elise asked Mary-Kate.

"What's wrong?" Mary-Kate said. "We spent two and a half hours in the shower last night washing pink stuff out of our hair. Her ears are water-logged!"

Ashley wiggled her earlobe. "That's better," she said. "Now, what did you want, Mary-Kate?"

"Never mind." Mary-Kate sighed. She glanced over at the next table. She tried to catch Campbell's,

Wendy's, or Phoebe's eyes. But the three friends were busy squirting honey designs all over their oatmeal. They wouldn't even look her way!

Great, Mary-Kate thought glumly. *I'm making new friends—but I'm losing all my old ones!*

"Elise?" Mary-Kate asked. "Don't you think we could ask Campbell, Phoebe, and—"

"Okay, you guys!" Elise interrupted. "It's time to tell you all about your next challenge."

Mary-Kate's shoulders dropped. Elise kept ducking the question about her friends. What was her problem?

"This challenge is top secret, so listen carefully," Elise told the twins in a low voice. "You see those portraits behind us? Of the ex-Heads?"

Mary-Kate glanced over her shoulder. The wall was covered with oil paintings of past head-mistresses since 1896. The women wore different hairstyles and fashions. But they had one thing in common: They all looked very serious!

"What about them?" Ashley asked.

"That's your next Glitter Girls challenge," Elise said excitedly. "Make those portraits look . . . funny!"

Mary-Kate thought *she* had water in her ears. Did she hear right? "We can't ruin those portraits!" she gasped.

"Who said anything about *ruining* them?" Elise said. "Do something funny with them. You'll think of something."

"Sure we will!" Ashley said cheerfully. "Right, Mary-Kate?"

"Right," Mary-Kate mumbled. But she wasn't so sure. As far as Elise's challenges went—this one topped them all!

"I'm telling you, Ashley," Mary-Kate whispered in the library during study period. "I'm worried!"

"About our next challenge?" Ashley asked.

"About our *friends*," Mary-Kate said. "If we don't tell Campbell, Wendy, and Phoebe about this club soon, they'll end up ditching *us!*"

"It's not going to happen," Ashley said. "Elise is waiting for the right time to invite them, that's all."

"Like when?" Mary-Kate scoffed. "When they're not speaking to us anymore?"

"Mary-Kate!" Ashley protested. "I thought you liked Elise. You said yourself that she was fun!"

"She is," Mary-Kate admitted. "But I'm beginning to think she's a bit of a flake."

"A flake who can get us tickets for the 4-You concert," Ashley pointed out.

"Shh!" Mrs. Winston, the librarian, warned.

The twins ducked behind the books they were holding. "Now, what are we going to do to the portraits?" Ashley whispered to Mary-Kate.

"Draw mustaches on them?" Mary-Kate suggested.

"Don't even go there, Mary-Kate!" Ashley hissed. "That would be ruining them!"

"Just a suggestion." Mary-Kate sighed. Her eyes drifted around the library. Suddenly she spotted a book propped up on a special stand. The gold title read: *White Oak, A Century of Headmistresses*!

"Bingo!" Mary-Kate said. She picked up the book and carried it back to their table. "There must be something we can do with this."

Mary-Kate and Ashley took turns flipping the pages. Each chapter featured a picture of a different headmistress and a full description.

"Check out Lucretia Tolliver," Mary-Kate said. "It says she owned two cocker spaniels that she brought to school every day."

"I hope they liked oatmeal!" Ashley giggled. She turned a page and began to read. "Wow! Mrs. Constance Hadley started the school newspaper in 1905. It says it had articles, short stories, and cartoons."

Cartoons? A lightbulb flashed inside Mary-Kate's head. "Ashley, that's it!" she said. "We can stick *cartoons* of the headmistresses over their *real* portraits!"

"But we can't draw!" Ashley protested.

"We don't have to," Mary-Kate said. "Campbell has a caricature program in her computer. All we do is scan these photographs and the computer turns them into goofy cartoons. I've fooled around with it a couple of times, so I've got the hang of it!"

"Then what are we waiting for?" Ashley whispered. "Let's go for it!"

Mary-Kate smiled. She was starting to have fun again. But there was still a problem. . . .

"How do we stick the cartoons on the portraits without ruining them?" Mary-Kate asked.

"I know!" Ashley said. "We can use Safe-Stick. It's tape that sticks without damaging surfaces."

"Good thinking, Ashley," Mary-Kate said. "Now all we have to do is check out this book and boot up Campbell's computer."

"Sure." Ashley sighed. "The hard part will be sneaking into the dining hall tonight to hang up our masterpieces!"

"You guys are totally brilliant!" Elise said at breakfast the next morning. "The Heads look like something out of a Saturday-morning cartoon!"

Mary-Kate beamed as she ate her blueberry muffin. Practically all of the White Oak girls were standing in front of the headmistresses' portraits, laughing and pointing. The crazy caricatures were a big hit!

"Do you think we'll get in trouble?" Ashley asked. "I mean, what if they trace the cartoons to the computer in Mary-Kate's room?"

"Don't worry," Cheryl said. Her gold glitter nail polish sparkled as she waved her hand. "Lots of girls have that cartoon program in their computers."

Mary-Kate looked over her shoulder. Campbell, Wendy, and Phoebe were staring at the portraits and giggling, too.

"Elise?" Ashley asked. "Don't you think it's time to invite Campbell, Wendy, and Phoebe to join the club?"

"Let's talk about those three later," Elise said. She wiggled excitedly in her seat. "Here comes the Head!"

Mary-Kate snapped around. Mrs. Pritchard was marching into the dining room. She was followed by Mrs. Bromsky, the dining hall lady, and a few assorted teachers.

The crowd of students parted as Mrs. Pritchard walked straight to the portraits. Just then Mary-Kate saw something that made her blood run cold. A trail of Sensational Strawberry glitter—yesterday's color—led right to Lucretia Tolliver's portrait!

"Hmmm," Mrs. Pritchard said as she slowly walked along the wall of portraits. "I seeeee."

Suddenly Mrs. Pritchard covered her mouth with her hand. Her shoulders began to move up and down.

"Look, Mary-Kate," Ashley whispered. "Mrs. Pritchard's laughing. She thinks the cartoons are funny!"

But when Mrs. Pritchard reached her own portrait she turned a deep shade of red. Pulling the paper down, she cleared her throat and faced the students.

"Okay, girls, we've all had a good chuckle," Mrs. Pritchard said. "But the next time you want to display your masterpieces, wait until our art show in the spring."

Mary-Kate watched Mrs. Pritchard walk toward the door. "And one more thing," Mrs. Pritchard said as she walked out. "I would like to see Ashley and Mary-Kate Burke in my office as soon as possible."

Oh, no, Mary-Kate thought. *We've been caught!*

CHAPTER NINE

Ashley felt sick as all eyes in the dining hall turned to her and Mary-Kate. How did Mrs. Pritchard find out that they did it? Did they drop a trail of glitter near the portraits? Did the librarian trace the headmistress book to them? Did they leave fingerprints?

Ashley could see Dana at the next table. She was eating a muffin and smiling slyly at her and Mary-Kate.

"Hey, I'm sorry if you two are in trouble," Elise shrugged. "But you should have been more careful."

"Are you for real?" Mary-Kate cried. "This whole thing was your idea!"

"Forget it, Mary-Kate." Ashley sighed. "Let's just

go to Mrs. Pritchard's office and get this over with."

"Good luck!" Summer said cheerfully.

The walk to the Main House was the longest Ashley had ever taken. By the time they reached Mrs. Pritchard's office, Ashley's heart was beating like a steel drum.

"Mary-Kate, Ashley?" Joan, Mrs. Pritchard's secretary, said. "Mrs. Pritchard will see you now."

Ashley took a deep breath and followed Mary-Kate into Mrs. Pritchard's office. The Head was sitting behind her big mahogany desk, looking over some papers. She glanced up and took off her reading glasses.

"You wanted to see us?" Ashley squeaked.

"Yes," Mrs. Pritchard said. She folded her hands on her desk. Then she smiled. "Congratulations, Ashley. You have been chosen to bake a cake for my annual tea."

Ashley's ears began to ring. She felt her knees weaken. "E-e-excuse me?" she stammered.

"Ms. Nesbitt told me what a fine cook you are," Mrs. Pritchard said. She turned to Mary-Kate. "And I thought you'd like to hear your sister's good news, too, Mary-Kate."

"Oh, it's *great* news, Mrs. Pritchard!" Mary-Kate said.

"The tea is this Saturday afternoon, Ashley," Mrs. Pritchard said. "So you're permitted to use the Culinary Arts classroom all Saturday morning."

"Thank you, Mrs. Pritchard!" Ashley said. "Is there anything special you'd like me to bake?"

"Surprise me," Mrs. Pritchard said. "I'm sure you're good at that. Now, don't be late for your next class!"

The twins hurried out of the office. When they were in the hall they leaned against the wall and sighed.

"Congratulations," Mary-Kate said.

"Thanks!" Ashley said. "That was so close!"

"Yeah," Mary-Kate said. "But we're not safe yet. Mrs. Pritchard might not know who made those caricatures. But we left a trail behind us—of pink glitter! And if Mrs. Pritchard didn't notice, you can bet someone else did!"

"Hey, you two!" Elise called out the next morning after morning announcements.

Ashley turned to see Elise pushing through the crowd of students. She was tugging another First Form girl by the hand. They were both wearing the glitter color of the day— Hi-Ho Silver!

"The others went ahead to the dining hall to save

us some muffins," Elise said. "In the meantime, meet Amber Fleming, our new Glitter Girl pledge!"

Ashley stared at Amber, then at Mary-Kate. She knew her sister was thinking the same thing she was—Why was Amber asked to join before Campbell, Wendy, and Phoebe?

"Um, Elise?" Ashley started to say.

"Amber can't wait to be a Glitter Girl," Elise went on. "In fact, she's already memorized the glitter colors for the entire week. Hit it, Amber!"

Amber counted on her hand. "Mondays it's Bodacious Blue, Tuesdays it's Groovy Green, Wednesdays it's—"

Ashley motioned Elise aside. "I think you should know that we left a trail of glitter at the portraits," she said.

"Big deal," Elise said. "As long as *Dana* didn't notice it, you're okay."

"Did someone say my name?"

Ashley gulped as she spun around. Dana and her friend Kristin had sneaked up behind them!

"Hi, Dana," Ashley said flatly.

"Good morning," Dana said. She pointed directly at Mary-Kate's left sneaker. "Is that pink glitter I see?"

"What are you talking about?" Mary-Kate asked.

She lifted her foot and there it was—powdered all over the bottom of her foot.

"Now, how did that get there?" Ashley asked.

"As if you didn't know!" Dana sneered. "Funny thing, that's the same color glitter I saw near the Heads' portraits. I think I'm starting to figure the whole thing out. You're all part of some club, aren't you? A club with initiations—"

Dana stopped cold when Elise pulled out a small plastic bag. Inside was the tainted oatmeal cookie.

"Want a cookie, Dana?" Elise asked, swinging the bag in front of her face. "It's got just the right amount of . . . pepper!"

Dana seemed almost hypnotized as she stared at the swinging bag. Then she knocked the bag away.

"Don't think you can keep getting away with it!" Dana warned. "Come on, Kristin. Let's go to the dining hall."

Kristin stuck her chin in the air and followed Dana out of the auditorium.

"This is getting hairy!" Mary-Kate complained. "I'm not sure I want to go on with this, Elise."

Ashley gasped. Her sister couldn't be thinking of quitting—not when they were so close!

"Don't stop now," Elise said with a smile. "You just have one little challenge left!"

Ashley gave Mary-Kate a pleading look. When that didn't seem to work, she began humming "In Your Face" by 4-You.

"Okay, okay." Mary-Kate sighed. "What do we do next?"

"Your next challenge is to glitterize Phoebe's side of the room," Elise said. "Is that a kick or what?"

Silence.

"Glitterize it?" Ashley asked.

Elise waved her hands in the air. "Yeah, you know—splash glitter all over her things! Her desk, her bed—"

Ashley couldn't believe what she had just heard!

"I could never do that!" Ashley declared. "Phoebe is my friend and roommate, and she hates glitter!"

"And why *Phoebe*?" Mary-Kate wanted to know.

Ashley thought she knew. "Elise?" Ashley asked. "Do you want us to do this because Phoebe refused to write that article about you?"

"No way!" Elise said with a laugh. "I just thought it would be funny, that's all."

"I can't do it, Elise," Ashley said. She could feel Mary-Kate moving closer to her for support.

Elise stared at Ashley. But then she shrugged. "That's okay," she said. "I was just thinking that you two deserve a break. I'll tell you your final challenge at our next meeting. It's after dinner in the laundry room."

"Why the laundry room?" Mary-Kate asked.

"Because nobody ever goes there," Elise said. "When was the last time you did your laundry?"

Ashley was embarrassed to say that she did her laundry every Sunday night—and ironed it, too!

"We'll be there," Ashley said.

"And another thing," Elise said. She gave a little jump. "I'm going to make a blockbuster announcement at the meeting. So be there at eight—and don't be late. And bring flashlights, too!"

Ashley watched as Elise and Amber hurried toward the dining hall. She had a good idea what the announcement would be. "This is it, Mary-Kate!" she said. "Elise is going to announce that she can get tickets to 4-You!"

"Then what are the flashlights for?" Mary-Kate asked.

"Maybe she wants to shine a spotlight on them!" Ashley giggled. "You know, like—Ta-daaaa!"

"Well, it's about time!" Mary-Kate said. "After what we've been through, we deserve front-row seats, backstage passes, and round-trip tickets to Japan!"

Ashley had trouble paying attention in her math and science classes. All morning she kept thinking about the upcoming meeting—and the surprise tickets!

When midday break finally came, Ashley headed to her room to drop off her books. But when she opened the door, she gasped. Phoebe's whole side of the room glowed like a float in a parade!

Oh, no, Ashley thought as she spun slowly around the room. There was sparkling blue glitter everywhere—on Phoebe's dresser, her bed, even all over her beloved posters of William Shakespeare and Emily Dickinson!

Who did this? Ashley wondered in a panic.

Just then Phoebe walked out from behind her wicker screen. "Nice job, Ashley," she said. Her mouth was a tight, thin line, and her glasses seemed to be steamed up.

"Phoebe, I did not do this," Ashley insisted.

"Oh, really?" Phoebe asked. She waved her arms around the room. "This glitter is exactly the same color as your dusting powder. Blue Star Dust, I believe?"

Ashley gulped. "Blue . . . Moon."

"And you *have* struck before," Phoebe said, pointing to her book of poetry on the shelf. "First my poetry book and now my whole side of the room. What next?"

Ashley moved closer to Phoebe. "I can explain, Phoebe," she said. "I mean, I will. One of these days!"

"One of these days?" Phoebe cried. "I knew you were acting weird lately. But I thought we were still friends."

Ashley felt a thick lump in the back of her throat. "We *are* still friends, Phoebe," she said. "Good friends!"

"Could have fooled me," Phoebe muttered. She took a small whisk broom out of her closet and began sweeping the glitter off of her dresser. "Now, if you don't mind, I just want to be left alone!"

Ashley backed out of their room and quietly closed the door. Leaning against the door, Ashley shut her eyes. She had never felt so torn in her life. What was more important—the 4-You concert or her friends?

Just one more challenge to go, Ashley thought. *Then we'll get those tickets and talk Elise into letting our friends join, too.*

Then everything will be back to normal.
I hope!

CHAPTER TEN

"Who could have done it, Mary-Kate?" Ashley asked later as they hurried to the meeting. She carried her flashlight at her side. "Who could have glitterized Phoebe's things?"

"A Glitter Girl—who else?" Mary-Kate said, swinging her flashlight. "But the question is—which one?"

"Hey, Mary-Kate!" Campbell's voice called out.

Mary-Kate and Ashley stopped and turned around. Campbell was standing in the hallway wearing a Yankees cap and jersey. A bag of corn chips was tucked under her arm.

"Hi, Campbell," Mary-Kate said. "What are you doing?"

"What am I doing?" Campbell asked, surprised. "The first play-offs are tonight. We were supposed to watch them together, remember?"

Mary-Kate gave her forehead a light whack. She and Campbell had planned to watch the baseball play-offs together two weeks ago!

"I forgot!" Mary-Kate admitted. "I guess I was kind of busy—"

"With your other friends!" Campbell finished. She pointed to the flashlights. "Going camping instead?"

Mary-Kate didn't know what to say. Instead she forced herself to smile. "What's the score?" she asked.

"Why don't you ask Elise?" Campbell muttered.

"Great," Mary-Kate said as Campbell walked down the hall. "Not only am I missing the play-offs, but I'm about to lose my best friend at White Oak."

"Why don't we ask Elise about Campbell, Wendy, and Phoebe again tonight?" Ashley suggested. "Right after she tells us about the 4-You tickets!"

"Okay," Mary-Kate said. "Tonight I'm getting an answer—once and for all."

"The meeting of the Glitter Girls will now come to order!" Elise announced.

The laundry room was dark. Everyone's faces looked ghostly as they stared at one another over their flashlights.

"Why are the lights out, Elise?" Cheryl asked. "What's up your sleeve this time?"

"You'll see!" Elise giggled. "But first may I just say that our new pledge, Amber, passed her first challenge with flying colors!"

"Blue Moon Dust to be exact!" Amber said with a smile.

"Blue Moon Dust?" Ashley repeated. "That's the color of my dusting powder."

So that's who glitterized Phoebe's side of the room, Mary-Kate thought. *Amber!*

Mary-Kate could tell her sister was struggling to keep her mouth shut. And for Ashley, that wasn't easy!

"Now for *my* big surprise!" Elise announced.

"This is it," Ashley whispered to Mary-Kate, "4-You, here we come!"

Mary-Kate watched as Elise reached into her pocket. Maybe Ashley was right. Maybe they *were* concert tickets.

"Ta-daaa!" Elise said. She held up a small, long, flat package. "Check it out!"

Mary-Kate shined her flashlight on the object. It

didn't look a concert ticket. It looked like . . . a pack of gum!

"It's called Chomp 'n' Glow!" Elise said, her eyes shining. "The first glitter bubble gum in history!"

The twins stared at the gum while Cheryl, Summer, and Amber oohed and aahed.

"Glitter bubble gum at last!" Samantha swooned.

"Now we can blow *and* glow at the same time!" Cheryl cheered. "All right!"

"That's why I wanted it pitch-black in here," Elise said. "So we could see if it glows in the dark or not!"

Everyone was quiet as Elise passed out sticks of Chomp 'n' Glow. Mary-Kate stuck one in her mouth and chewed. The strong cherry flavor reminded her of cough medicine.

"As soon as you feel a bubble coming on, switch off your flashlight," Elise ordered. "Any questions?"

"Just one," Ashley said, trying to be polite. "How about Campbell, Phoebe, and Wendy joining the club? You said you'd think about it."

"I did think about it," Elise said.

"*And?*" Mary-Kate and Ashley asked at the same time.

"And I'm sorry to say I don't think they're Glitter

Girls material," Elise said with a shrug.

The words hit Mary-Kate like a thunderbolt. Who was Elise Van Hook to judge her friends like that?

She had been right all along. Elise had no intention of asking her friends to join the Glitter Girls.

And if Campbell, Phoebe, and Wendy couldn't join, Mary-Kate didn't want to, either!

Jumping up, Mary-Kate switched on the laundry-room light. Everyone protested and covered their eyes.

"Mary-Kate, what are you doing?" Elise cried.

"I need some water," Mary-Kate said. "This gum tastes like it was double-chewed and spit out!"

"But Chomp 'n' Glow is the new regulation bubble gum of the Glitter Girls," Elise protested. "You have to like it!"

"No I don't," Mary-Kate said, walking toward the door. "Because I'm not a Glitter Girl."

"You mean, *yet*!" Elise corrected.

"No, I mean, *never*!" Mary-Kate declared. "I quit!"

CHAPTER ELEVEN

"Why is there cinnamon in my oatmeal?" Elise demanded at breakfast the next day.

"That's not cinnamon, it's glitter from your eye shadow," Amber pointed out. "Saturday's color is Rickaracka Firecracker Red—"

"I knew that!" Elise interrupted.

Ashley twirled her spoon in her oatmeal. Sitting at the Glitter Girls' table wasn't the same without Mary-Kate. Ashley didn't blame her sister for quitting. She was mad at Elise, too, for not letting their friends join the club. But she wanted those 4-You concert tickets—and she wanted them bad!

"So, Ashley," Elise said. "Did you try to talk Mary-Kate out of quitting?"

"I tried," Ashley admitted. "But once Mary-Kate makes up her mind, that's it."

"Wow!" Summer said. "She must have really hated that bubble gum!"

Elise looked disappointed as she took a sip of her orange juice. "I really wanted you both to join."

"I did, too," Ashley admitted. "But I'm still in. In fact, I'm already up for my last challenge."

"Cool!" Elise said. "Because you're really going to like this one!"

"How come?" Ashley asked.

Elise shrugged. "Because everyone knows you're the best baker in the First Form," she said. "What we want you to do is bake a gross cake for Mrs. Pritchard's tea today!"

Ashley laughed nervously. "Very funny, you guys."

"It's not a joke," Elise insisted. "The gross cake is your next and final challenge, Ashley!"

Ashley dropped her oatmeal spoon on the table with a clang. They *were* serious!

"I can't do that!" Ashley said. "I could get into major trouble!"

"Relax!" Cheryl said. "You saw how Mrs. Pritchard laughed at those cartoons you and Mary-Kate hung up the other day. She's cool!"

Ashley's head was spinning—the way it did when she swallowed ice cream too fast!

"Oh, come on, Ashley," Elise said. She raised her oatmeal spoon to make a point. "Tomorrow at this time you'll be a full-fledged Glitter Girl."

"You're so lucky, Ashley!" Amber sighed, her face dripping with peanut butter. "I still have a whole week of challenges left."

"Now, here's what you have to do," Elise went on. "Make the cake look like an ordinary chocolate cake on the outside. But on the inside—fill it with Tabasco and Worcestershire sauce!"

"I don't know if I can do it, Elise," Ashley groaned.

"Think about it." Elise shrugged. "In the meantime think about this. I just spoke to my parents in Japan. They said they could get you a front-row ticket to the 4-You concert in Chicago."

Ashley stared at Elise. The concert she'd been dreaming about was only one challenge away. And all she had to say was—

"Okay," Ashley blurted. "I'll do it!"

"What was I thinking?" Ashley wailed to herself in the Food Management Center.

It was Saturday afternoon, and Ashley had spent

over an hour stuffing a beautiful chocolate cake with hideously gross ingredients. Now the bogus cake was in the oven!

To make matters worse, Dana's friend Kristin had come into the kitchen earlier—just as Ashley was pouring Tabasco sauce into the cake mix!

"What are you doing in here?" Ashley had gasped.

"Getting lemons for my facial," Kristin had said, staring at the Tabasco sauce. "What are you doing, Ashley?"

Ashley had laughed nervously. "You don't expect me to reveal my secret recipe, do you?"

But Kristin hadn't been laughing. Her eyes had stayed glued to the Tabasco as she'd gotten her lemons and walked out the door.

Ashley shuddered. All Kristin would have to do was bust her—and the only ticket she'd get would be a one-way to Chicago!

The door opened and Ashley jumped. It was Mary-Kate!

I can't tell Mary-Kate about my latest challenge, Ashley thought. *Mary-Kate quit the Glitter Girls—she wouldn't understand!*

"H-hi, Mary-Kate," Ashley said.

"Hi, yourself!" Mary-Kate said with a grin. She was dressed in gray sweats and a Cubs cap. "I just wanted to see how you were doing. Today's the big day, you know!"

"I know," Ashley said.

Mary-Kate walked over to the counter, which was covered with pans and mixing bowls. She rubbed her hands together.

"Time to lick the bowl!" Mary-Kate said.

Ashley gasped as Mary-Kate dragged her finger along the ridge of the mixing bowl. "Get your hand out of there!" she shouted.

"But you always let me lick the bowl back home in Chicago!" Mary-Kate said. "It's practically a tradition!"

"It's not a tradition in New Hampshire!" Ashley grabbed the bowl back. "Give it back, Mary-Kate!"

"What's the matter?" Mary-Kate said. "Afraid I'll discover your secret recipe?"

Ashley tried to stop Mary-Kate, but it was too late. Her sister already had her finger in her mouth.

She watched in horror as Mary-Kate's eyes began to cross. Then her face turned tomato red!

"Blah!" Mary-Kate gagged. She dropped the plastic bowl on the floor. "What did you put in here—chili powder?"

"Just a pinch," Ashley said in a small voice. "Along with Tabasco . . . and a dash of Worcestershire."

"Tabasco and Worcestershire in a chocolate cake?" Mary-Kate shrieked. "Are you crackers?"

"As they say, variety is the spice of life," Ashley said. "So I used a variety . . . of spices!"

Mary-Kate looked at Ashley long and hard.

"Call it another twin thing, Ashley," Mary-Kate said. "But I know you're not telling me something."

Ashley sighed. She didn't want to tell Mary-Kate but she had no choice. "My final Glitter Girls challenge was to bake a gross cake for Mrs. Pritchard's tea. So I did."

A look of shock spread over Mary-Kate's face. "You mean this was all another initiation challenge?"

Ashley nodded. "Scary, isn't it?"

"Totally!" Mary-Kate cried. She gave Ashley's shoulders a shake. "Ashley, you're the one who's going to get in trouble—not them!"

"But I'm just one more challenge away from joining the club!" Ashley protested. "And going to the 4-You concert!"

"Ashley, no club is worth breaking the rules and losing friends," Mary-Kate said. "No matter how many concert tickets you can get!"

Ashley whipped off her apron and tossed it on the table. She was used to be being lectured by their dad and even by their baby-sitter, Carrie. But by her twin sister—it was a nightmare! What made it worse was that Mary-Kate was right!

"That's it." Ashley sighed. She slipped on a pair of oven mitts and ran to the oven. After switching off the heat, she opened the door and pulled out the cake. "I'm trashing this cake and baking a new one!" she announced. She placed the cake on the counter. "And right before I do that, I'm telling Elise that I quit, too!"

"Atta girl!" Mary-Kate cheered.

"There's only one other problem," Ashley said. "Kristin Lindquist came in before. She caught me pouring Tabasco sauce into the cake mix."

"Don't worry," Mary-Kate said. "As long as the cake doesn't get to Mrs. Pritchard, you're safe."

The twins left the gross cake on the counter and headed straight for Porter House. But as they hurried through the hall toward Elise's room, the dorm phone rang. Ashley stopped to pick it up.

"Porter House," Ashley said.

"Hello," a woman's voice said. "I would like to speak to my daughter, please. Her name is Elise Van Hook."

Elise? Ashley put her hand over the mouthpiece. "Guess what, Mary-Kate? It's Elise's concert promoter parents!"

"Here we go again," Mary-Kate muttered.

Ashley turned back to the phone. "Hi, Mrs. Van Hook. I'm Ashley Burke. And I'll bet you're calling from Japan."

"No," Mrs. Van Hook said. "I'm calling from Fiji. Mr. Van Hook and I are here with the Peace Corps."

"The Peace Corps?" Ashley asked excitedly. "Are they a hot new group? Have they been on MTV yet?"

There was a moment of silence. Then Mrs. Van Hook chuckled. "The Peace Corps is an organization that sends volunteers to underdeveloped countries. There they teach people how to plant, read, build wells—"

"And promote rock concerts?" Ashley broke in.

"Rock concerts?" Mrs. Van Hook laughed. "Honey, the only rocks around here are on the beach."

Ashley stared at the phone. "Elise didn't tell me you were in the Peace Corps," she said.

"We used to be tax lawyers," Mrs. Van Hook explained. "Now we're digging ditches and loving every minute of it!"

Ashley squeezed the handle on the receiver—hard. Everything Elise had told them about her parents was a lie!

CHAPTER TWELVE

"What's the matter?" Mary-Kate whispered. She shook Ashley's arm. "What did she say? What did she say?"

"Shh!" Ashley placed her finger to her lips. Then she smiled sweetly into the receiver. "I'll get Elise for you, Mrs. Van Hook. Please hold on."

Ashley let the receiver swing as she grabbed Mary-Kate. "Elise's parents are not concert promoters!" she said. "They're ex-tax lawyers and Peace Corps volunteers!"

"No way!" Mary-Kate cried. "Let's find Elise and tell her she has a phone call. We won't tell her what we know. Yet."

"You go," Ashley said. "I want to run and tell

Phoebe all about Elise and this stupid club. Once and for all."

"Why?" Mary-Kate asked.

"Because I want my friends back!" Ashley declared.

Mary-Kate nodded. She turned on her heel and sped down the hallway. Ashley ran down the stairs to her own room.

She found Phoebe sitting on the floor and scraping her vintage platform shoes with a nail file.

"Phoebe, what are you doing?" Ashley asked.

"What does it look like I'm doing?" Phoebe snapped. "I'm scraping blue glitter off my shoes. Glitter that you put there, thank you very much."

Ashley tilted her head. "Phoebe? Aren't those the shoes you got in the Saturday Night Fever auction?"

"Yes!" Phoebe snapped. "So?"

"So," Ashley said. "Didn't that pair already have blue glitter on it?"

Phoebe stared at the shoe in her hand. She sank back on her heels and sighed. "You're right." She sighed. "There's so much glitter around here, I don't know where it's coming from anymore!"

Ashley sat on the floor next to Phoebe. She took a deep breath and explained everything. About the secret club, the initiations, even the gross party cake!

"So that's why you slopped peanut butter on your face," Phoebe asked. "And messed up my room?"

"Yes and no," Ashley said. "You can blame the club for the peanut butter, but I never glitterized your side of the room!"

Phoebe raised an eyebrow. "You mean it?"

Ashley nodded. "Cross my heart and hope to croak. Drop a toenail in my Coke!"

"I believe you." Phoebe laughed.

Ashley wiggled closer to Phoebe. "Now here's a real bombshell," she said. "Elise's parents were never concert promoters in the first place. They used to be tax lawyers and now they're Peace Corps volunteers!"

Phoebe jumped up. "That's great!"

Ashley wrinkled her nose. "It is?"

Phoebe's glasses wiggled as she nodded hard. "They quit their high-paying jobs to help those less fortunate? How romantic! How noble!" She swooned.

Ashley shrugged. She never thought of it that way. But now that Phoebe mentioned it . . .

"I am going to write a few lines about Elise in the school paper," Phoebe said. "I'll call it 'Introducing Elise Van Hook,' and I'll mention her fabulous mom and dad. Don't you think she'll love it?"

Ashley smiled. "Oh, she'll flip, all right."

"Good," Phoebe said. "If I write it right away, I can get it into this week's edition."

The door opened and Mary-Kate walked into the room. "Elise is on the phone now," she said. "I still can't believe how she lied to us!"

"Me either," Ashley said. "Out of all the fibs I've ever heard, this one takes the cake!"

THE CAKE!

Ashley's eyes flew open. "The bogus cake is still in the Food Management Center!" she cried. "I have to trash it before someone sneaks a lick!"

The twins raced out of Porter House and straight to the Food Management Center. But when they walked inside the classroom, the cake was gone!

"Where'd it go?" Ashley wondered out loud.

Ms. Nesbitt walked into the classroom and smiled. "Oh, Ashley," she said. "I found your chocolate cake sitting on the counter and took it to Mrs. Pritchard's office."

"Y-you what?" Ashley stammered.

"Don't worry," Ms. Nesbitt said. "It's safely in her fridge. Where no one can sneak a taste!"

Ashley stared at her sister. Her worst nightmare was about to come true!

"Oh, and by the way," Ms. Nesbitt said as she

hung up her apron. "The teachers' tea starts in just two hours!"

There was dead silence as Ms. Nesbitt walked out of the classroom.

"Two hours to live!" Ashley moaned. "After Mrs. Pritchard sinks her teeth into that cake, she'll sink her teeth into us!"

Mary-Kate grabbed Ashley by the shoulders. "Snap out of it, Ashley!" she said. "All you have to do is sneak the bad cake out of Mrs. Pritchard's office and switch it with a new one!"

"Mary-Kate, do the math!" Ashley cried. "How can I bake a cake, cool it, and replace it in just two hours?"

Mary-Kate paced the classroom. "You're right," she said. "Baking a cake is not something you can do in an instant . . ."

"Instant!" she exclaimed. "Instant pudding!"

Ashley rolled her eyes. "Mary-Kate, I know that's all you can cook," she said. "But we can't serve instant pudding at Mrs. Pritchard's tea!"

"Not *just* instant pudding." Mary-Kate shook her head. "Remember that awesome Toffee Bar Crunch cake you once whipped up in Chicago? It was made with instant pudding and it took only an hour!"

Ashley nodded. "It *was* awesome! And I can get

all the ingredients from the class pantry," she said. "Mary-Kate, you're brilliant!"

Mary-Kate smiled as she planted her hands on her hips. "It's about time you noticed!" she joked.

The door swung open. Phoebe walked in wearing her pink-and-orange apron. She was followed by Wendy and Campbell—and they were all smiling!

"Phoebe told us what happened," Wendy told the twins. "We had no idea."

"I know." Ashley sighed. "And we're sorry about the whole thing."

"Anyway." Phoebe gave her apron a pat. "We thought you'd need some help here in the kitchen."

"Thanks, you guys!" Ashley said.

"Hey, don't mention it," Wendy said. "That's what friends are for."

The word made Ashley feel warm and fuzzy inside. After everything that happened—they were still friends!

"Okay, team," Ashley said. She rolled up the sleeves of her gray sweater. "Let's get cooking!"

The girls measured, chopped, mixed, and poured. The cake took only one hour to make!

"It's a masterpiece!" Phoebe swooned.

Ashley felt an excited shiver down her back. She

carefully picked up the toffee cake and took a deep breath. "Let the switch begin."

Mary-Kate, Campbell, Phoebe, and Wendy surrounded Ashley as they walked out of the Food Management Center and through the campus. When they reached the Main Building, Mrs. Pritchard's office was unlocked and empty.

Mary-Kate opened the small refrigerator behind Mrs. Pritchard's desk. There was the bogus chocolate cake. She yanked it out and placed it on a cabinet behind Mrs. Pritchard's desk.

"Quick, Ashley," Mary-Kate hissed. "Put the good cake in the fridge. Now!"

Ashley quickly slid the toffee cake into the fridge. She was about to shut the refrigerator door when . . .

"Girls!" a frosty voice called.

Mary-Kate, Ashley, and their friends whirled around. Mrs. Pritchard was standing at the door with her hands on her hips. Standing right next to her was Dana Woletsky!

CHAPTER THIRTEEN

"I told you, Mrs. Pritchard," Dana said, her chin in the air. "Ashley trashed your cake with Tabasco sauce and now they're sneaking it into your fridge. It's all part of the plot!"

"Whoa, slow down, Dana," Mrs. Pritchard ordered. "How do you know Ashley tainted my cake?"

Dana folded her arms across her chest. "Because I have a *witness*!" she bragged.

Ashley was terrified. Dana had done it. She had finally gone through with her threat. She had told Mrs. Pritchard about the cake, and she would probably tell her about the club initiations, too!

From the corner of her eye, Ashley could see

Wendy, Phoebe, and Campbell standing shoulder-to-shoulder in front of the gross chocolate cake. A human shield!

"Is that the cake you baked for my tea, Ashley?" Mrs. Pritchard asked.

"Huh?" Ashley asked, her head snapping around.

"That cake." Mrs. Pritchard pointed to the toffee cake in the refrigerator. "Is that the one?"

"*Yes!*" Ashley and Mary-Kate said at the same time.

"Then let me taste it, please," Mrs. Pritchard said.

Ashley held her breath as she pulled the toffee cake out of the refrigerator. She kept holding her breath as Mrs. Pritchard took a fork out of her desk and stuck it in the cake.

"You'd better have a glass of water handy, Mrs. Pritchard," Dana warned. "You're going to need it."

The office was silent as Mrs. Pritchard tasted the cake.

"Mmm-mmm!" Mrs. Pritchard said. "There is absolutely nothing wrong with this cake. In fact—it's delicious!"

"What?" Dana cried.

"Thank you, Mrs. Pritchard!" Ashley gushed.

"But—Kristin saw it with her own eyes!" Dana

cried. "She saw Ashley pour Tabasco right into the—"

"Well, then maybe Kristin should mind her own business," Mrs. Pritchard interrupted. "And so should you, Dana!"

"B-but," Dana stammered. "But—"

"From now on, I don't want to hear any more false accusations," Mrs. Pritchard told Dana. "Now, please apologize to Ashley. Then go and enjoy your Saturday."

Dana's face glowed redder and redder. Her green eyes were so narrow they were practically slits!

"Sorry, Ashley," Dana snapped.

"Apology accepted, Dana," Ashley said. She could hear Mary-Kate snicker softly as Dana left the office.

"Well, now!" Mrs. Pritchard gave Ashley a little wink. "I knew you'd surprise me, Ashley. Now why don't you put the cake back in the fridge? I want it to be nice and cold for the tea."

Ashley couldn't believe her good luck. The Head would never see the gross chocolate cake after all. Amazing!

The day was full of surprises, all right. For *everyone*!

"Well?" Elise asked Ashley on Sunday morning. "How did the tea go? What shade of green did Mrs. Pritchard turn when she tasted your red-hot cake?"

Elise, Summer, Cheryl, and Samantha were waiting anxiously in front of Ashley's door.

"The tea?" Ashley asked. She peeked out from her door and yawned. Elise, Summer, Cheryl, and Samantha crowded in front of her door. "What tea?"

"Ashley, don't pretend!" Elise said. "We looked all over for you last night. Where were you?"

Ashley smiled as she stepped out of her room. She pulled a copy of the White Oak *Acorn* from behind her back.

"In the newsroom!" she declared. "Helping Phoebe write an article all about White Oak's newest First Form girl, Elise Van Hook!"

Elise shrieked happily and jumped up and down. Her friends did the same.

"You really did write it!" Elise said. She grabbed the paper from Ashley's hands and began to read out loud:

" 'If you already thought that Elise Van Hook was the shining new light at White Oak, check out her mom and dad. Once busy tax lawyers, the two selfless souls quit their jobs to become . . . to become . . . ' "

"Yeee-eeees?" Ashley said as Elise's face dropped.

Cheryl took the paper and continued to read:

" 'To become Peace Corps volunteers in Fiji'?"

"Peace corps?" Samantha gasped.

"Fiji?" Summer cried.

Elise's mouth opened but nothing came out. Ashley moved away from her door, and Mary-Kate stepped out.

"I guess your parents might have trouble getting us concert tickets, Elise," Mary-Kate said. "How about coconuts instead?"

"Very funny!" Elise snapped.

"Is it true, Elise?" Cheryl demanded. "Did you lie about your parents?"

Elise shrugged. "It wasn't really a lie," she said in a small voice. "More of . . . an exaggeration."

"Peace Corps volunteers and rock concert promoters?" Cheryl scoffed. "A bit of a stretch, if you ask me!"

"I can't believe we fell for it!" Summer groaned.

At first Elise looked as if she were about to panic. But then she took a long, deep breath and began to speak.

"Look, I'm sorry I lied," she said. "It's just that I was new and wanted to make friends. My old school was really competitive that way."

"So you made up the story about your parents

just to make friends?" Ashley asked.

"Sure," Elise said. "It worked with you, didn't it?"

Ashley nodded. It sure did!

"The club was another idea from my old school," Elise said. "They'd have initiations like you wouldn't believe. One time I had to wear a grubby baseball shirt and sweatpants to a formal dance!"

Mary-Kate shrugged. "That's bad?"

"The pits!" Elise complained. "So when I got to White Oak, I wanted to be the one who called the shots. I guess it was another one of my crazy ideas."

Elise gave the twins a small smile. "And I *was* going to let Phoebe, Campbell, and Wendy join," she said. "I just wanted the club to seem really selective at first."

At least she came clean, Ashley thought. *But there's still one thing I don't get . . .*

"How long could you have lied, Elise?" she asked. "Sooner or later we would have seen there were no tickets."

"Yeah, like—*duh*!" Cheryl said.

Elise nodded. "After I made enough friends, I would have made up an excuse about my parents."

"Like what?" Mary-Kate asked.

"I don't know." Elise shrugged. "Like they quit

their jobs to join the Peace Corps?"

Ashley felt sorry for Elise. She knew what it was like to be the new kid. And to want friends really badly.

"Now everyone will know my parents are boring," Elise said as she stared at the newspaper.

"Phoebe doesn't think your mom and dad are boring, Elise," Ashley said. "In fact, she wrote that their story would make an awesome movie."

"She did?" Elise looked down at the newspaper and grinned. "Hey—she did!"

Samantha, Summer, and Cheryl glanced over Elise's shoulder. They seemed interested again!

"Who do you think would play your dad?" Samantha asked. "Harrison Ford? Kevin Spacey?"

"How about Brendan Fraser?" Cheryl asked excitedly. "He's been in the jungle before!"

"And he looks great in a loincloth!" Summer added.

Ashley watched as Elise and her friends walked away, chattering the names of superstars.

"Okay." Ashley sighed. "Elise may not be the cool girl at White Oak anymore—but she sure knows how to liven things up."

"Yeah," Mary-Kate said. "And lucky for us, we survived all those challenges. Our pink hair dye came out. And we finally stopped smelling like pickles and peanut butter."

Miss Viola, the housemother, walked over to Mary-Kate and Ashley. "Excuse me, girls," she said. "But there are two Harrington boys outside the house waiting to see you."

Boys?

Ashley gave a little jump. "I'll bet it's Ross!"

"And a *friend*!" Mary-Kate said excitedly.

The twins charged down the stairs. But once outside they came face-to-face with . . .

"The Nunzio twins!" Ashley groaned.

"Yo!" Andrew said with a grin. He waved the twins' note in his hand. "We got your poem a few days ago. Looks like you girls are diggin' us!"

"It was pretty gross at first," Arthur admitted. "But now we're ready for looooove!"

The Nunzio twins pursed their lips and made sloppy kissing noises. Mary-Kate looked at Ashley and groaned.

"Looks like I spoke too soon!" Mary-Kate whispered.

"Yeah." Ashley sighed. "*Way* too soon!"

ACORN

The Voice of White Oak Academy Since 1905

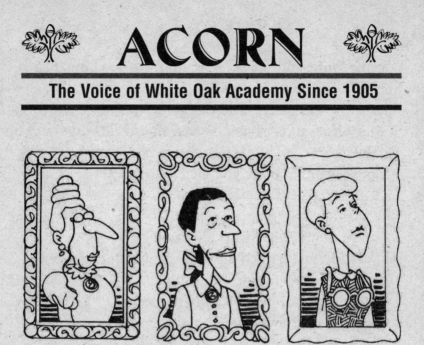

Look what's happened to our headmistresses! From left to right: Miss Chatham, Miss Tolliver, and Mrs. Pritchard.

HEADS UP!
by Phoebe Cahill

News flash! All the White Oak headmistresses have turned into cartoons! That's right, folks. Sometime during the dark of night someone pasted kooky caricatures over all the portraits of the headmistresses in the dining hall. White Oak's morning oatmeal will never be the same!

Picture it—now Penelope Chatham's nose is as big as Pinocchio's! And Lucretia Tolliver's mouth is as wide as the Grand Canyon! Amazing! (And whatever happened to Mrs. Pritchard's chin? I hope she has a good sense of humor!)

Who were the master-minds behind this plot? Why did they carry it out? And where will they strike next?

No one knows—or at least no one's talking. (Did anyone else notice a suspicious trail of pink glitter on the floor of the dining hall?) In the meantime, keep your eyes peeled for more signs of mischief. Something tells me this is just the beginning!

GLAM GAB
by Ashley Burke
and Phoebe Cahill

Fashion maven Ashley Burke

What's the hottest fashion trend today? Styles from the groovin' seventies. Bell-bottoms, platform boots—and tie-dyeing! The cool thing about tie-dyeing is that you can do it yourself. We made our own fab tie-dyed shirts—right here in Potter House. You can, too. Here's how:

You will need: 1) a cotton T-shirt; 2) dyes from a craft store or kit; 3) rubber bands; 4) rubber gloves; 5) plastic trash bag; 6) bucket or sink.

A. Saturate the T-shirt in tap water and then wring it dry.

B. Roll or pleat the shirt into a long tube. Tie with rubber bands at two-inch intervals.

C. Soak the bundle in hot tap water in a sink or bucket for 20 minutes. Add a cup of salt. This will help the dye set better.

D. Put on rubber gloves (and maybe an apron). Squirt the dye into the fabric between the bands. Make sure the dye gets into the folds, too. Wash your hands and work area before adding each new color.

E. Put the bundle into a plastic trash bag and let it sit for 24 hours.

F. Put on the gloves and rinse the bundle under tap water until the water runs clear. Cut off the

rubber bands.

G. Wash the shirt in a washing machine with hot water, then hang dry.

Far out! You've made your very own genuine tie-dyed shirt. Enjoy!

Ashley and Phoebe

THE GET-REAL GIRL

Dear Get-Real Girl,
There's a guy at the Harrington School who is all that and more! I know his whole schedule, what he likes to eat, and his favorite music group (Matchbox Twenty). There's just one major problem—he doesn't even know I'm alive! How can I make him notice me? HELP!

Signed,
Pining at Porter

Dear Pining,
There are loads of ways to make him notice you. You can accidentally step on his toe with a pair of deadly cha-cha heels, or bump into him while carrying a double-chocolate fudge pop on a stick, or show up at the next White Oak/Harrington event in a Hefty bag. Or you can just go up to him and say "hi." You can even talk about Matchbox

Twenty's last album. And if he still doesn't talk to you—*then* you can acciden-

tally step on his toe with your cha-cha heels! Good luck!

Signed,
Get-Real Girl

Dear Get-Real Girl,
My roommate is a total slob! The other day I came home and found an open bag of chips spilling onto her bed! Her dirty clothes pile is so high it's casting a shadow over my comput-er! She even airs out her stinky sneakers on the windowsill—next to my budding African violet plants! What should I do?

Signed,
Grossed Out in
New Hampshire

Dear Grossed Out,
All I've got to say is—get real! Who were you hop-ing to room with—Mr. Clean? And as long as your roomie offers you some of her chips, who cares if they've taken the place of her bedspread? But okay, okay, if finding pretzels in your slippers is getting to be too much, here's a tip. Sit down with your roomie and tell her how you feel. Then offer to help her

shop for plastic contain-ers to hold her crunchy-munchies. And if that doesn't work—mention you saw a giant cock-roach crawling on her toothbrush. That ought to do it!

Signed,
Get-Real Girl

Kick it Up!
White Oak Squirrels KO Cresthaven!
by Mary-Kate Burke

What better way to start the new school year than

Sports pro Mary-Kate Burke

with a major win? That's what happened when the White Oak Squirrels went against the First Form soccer team from the Cresthaven School.

Things looked pretty bleak for White Oak during the first half. Cheryl Miller and Veronica Soto saw stars when they went for the same head ball! Midfielder Tammy Mazzaferro caused a scene when she kicked the ball into the wrong net!

But after half-time White Oak came through. Big time! Defender Lisa Dunmead scored a goal. So did sweeper Tomika Carson. But the real high point came when Campbell Smith scored not one, not two, but three goals, breaking the tie and winning the game for White Oak!

After the awesome victory, the Squirrels celebrated with pizza and punch and named Campbell Most Valuable Player. But to me she'll always be MER— Most Excellent Roommate! Go Campbell!

THE FIRST FORM BUZZ
by Dana Woletsky

Fall is here and the air is crisp with back-to-school excitement. (Maybe it has to do with all the boys on campus. Have you seen the new hottie in bio lab?) The air is also buzzing with gossip, gossip, gossip!!

For starters, WHO'S GOT THE CAT? It seems that the NO PETS AT WHITE OAK rule has not stopped a First Former in the Phipps Dorm! How do I

know? Sources tell me that the sounds of a cat scratching have been heard on the third floor. Either that, or SVS has been filing her nails in the middle of the night again. . . . And they call me catty!

Here's some more hot gossip for you—red hot! A certain twin with the initials AB was seen adding Tabasco sauce to what

seemed to be the cake for the annual teacher's tea! I would pass on all chocolate cake from now until winter break. And watch out for AB—she brings new meaning to the words Spice Girl!

Oh, well. Gotta sign off. Another First Form twin with the initials MKB is pestering me for the computer. Something about a soccer article. But before I buzz off, remember this— If you want the scoop, you just gotta snoop!

The Buzz Girl

Upcoming Calendar— Fall/Winter

•On your mark, get set, chaaaaarge it! The next mall shopping spree will be Saturday, October 16th at 10:30 AM. So get ready to shop till you drop!

•There's no place like Homecoming—especially when it means the first White Oak/Harrington dance of the semester! So circle Friday, October 22nd and get ready to party on!

•Hear those Harrington boys before their voices change! Come to the next Glee Club concert at the Performing Arts Center on Sunday, Nov. 15th, 3:00 PM. Singing isn't just for showers anymore!

•Wannabe superstars— now's your chance to shine! Auditions for the White Oak Academy musical will be held right after Halloween. Go for it!

•Put on those high-top snowshoes and head for the White Oak/Harrington Winter Festival the weekend of January 29-31. The weather may be frightful but Mrs. Pritchard's hot cocoa is always dee-light-ful!

It's All in the Stars
Fall Horoscopes

Virgo:
(Aug. 23-Sept. 22)

Get ready for a new Fall term-and a new life! Open yourself up to possibilities (and don't let your tendency to worry hold you back). Who knows what's around the corner: a facinating class, a cool friend, or a fabulous guy?

Libra:
(Sept. 23-Oct. 22)

Forget the balancing act—and go for it! Want to get to know that cute new boy in history class? Talk to him! Want to make the basketball team? Shoot some hoops! Want the lead in the new school musical? Practice, practice, practice! Remember: You can do it! (And if you don't get the lead, you can still have a great time in the chorus.)

Scorpio:
(Oct. 23-Nov. 21)

'Tis the season to make new friends—and keep the old. You know how much you care about your best buds—so why not show it? Make time to do fun things with your friends. Listen to their problems. Laugh at their jokes. And once in a while—get everyone together for a party and spring for the pizza. Enjoy!

PSST! Take a sneak peek
at

TWO of a kind™ #13

War of the Wardrobes

"Say it's not true," Ashley Burke begged. "Please—tell me it's a joke. Just a cruel, ugly joke. We can't be getting school uniforms!"

Wendy Linden shook her head. "It's no joke. Everyone at White Oak Academy will have uniforms by the end of the month. My mom said so."

Ashley rolled her eyes and glanced at her friends. White Oak Academy was the best—but not if she had to wear uniforms!

"So what are we going to do about it?" Mary-Kate asked.

"What *can* we do?" Phoebe said.

"We can protest!" Elise suggested. "I say we all

98

wear pajamas to class tomorrow! That will let the Head know that we won't put up with this new policy."

Protest? Ashley thought. She and Mary-Kate exchanged glances. Did they really want to get caught up in another one of Elise's schemes?

No way, Ashley decided. *Elise is fun, but her ideas are a little too far out.*

But then Ashley caught the look on Phoebe's face. Her eyes had lit up at the word.

"Protest!" Phoebe cried. "What a great idea! It's so totally retro. And besides—I've got a great vintage nightgown and robe."

"I don't know," Wendy argued. "I'm not sure we'll get very far that way. I mean, if we show up for class in pajamas, won't the Head be even more determined to make us wear uniforms?"

"And besides," Mary-Kate chimed in, "tomorrow we're going to Harrington—remember?"

"Good point," Ashley said.

"So?" Elise asked. "What's the problem?"

"I don't want to parade around in my jams in front of the guys," Mary-Kate declared.

"Why not?" Elise asked. "I bet the guys will think it's cool."

"Have you seen her pj's?" Ashley cracked. "Not

exactly a fashion statement. She sleeps in a Chicago Bulls T-shirt every night."

"What's wrong with that?" Mary-Kate challenged her sister.

"Nothing. It's just that it's shorter than my shortest skirt," Ashley argued. "You'll freeze!"

"Okay, fine," Elise said to Mary-Kate. "You can chicken out if you want to. But I'm doing it. I'm organizing this pajama protest."

Then Elise turned to Ashley. "Well, Ashley—what about it? Do you really want to just cave in to school uniforms? Just sit back and let the administration tell us what to wear—without saying a word?"

Do I? Ashley wondered. That didn't sound like her.

Suddenly she had an idea. A brilliant idea.

"No," Ashley said. "I'm going to do something about it."

"What?" Elise asked.

Ashley smiled. "Just wait until the school newspaper comes out next week," she said. "Then you'll see!"

Listen To Us!

Greatest Hits

Ballet Party™

Birthday Party™

Sleepover Party™

Brother For Sale™

Mary-Kate & Ashley's CDs and
Cassettes Available Now
Wherever Music is Sold

I Am The Cute One™